In memory of Kamilek from Częstochowa, a bright soul lost too soon, may this book carry the timeless message of resilience to all children.

May it inspire a world where every child feels safe, loved, and free to dream.

Copyright 2023 Dagmara Sitek

All rights reserved. This book or any portion thereof may not be reproduced or used in any manner without the expressed written permission of the publisher except for the use of brief quotations in a book review.

ISBN: 978-1-7381285-2-5 (Paperback)

ISBN: 978-1-7381285-1-8 (Hardcover)

All inquiries about this book can be sent to the author at info@couragetales.com

For more information, or to book an event, visit my website: www.couragetales.com

Loris Opens Up His Heart

Dagmara Sitek

Illustrated By
Lau Frank

Unfortunately, the next few days didn't get any better.

"Would you like a hot dog?"

"No."

Loris had been in and out in different foster homes.

"Time to leave. Again."

"Don't worry, we'll find you! And we'll bring an umbrella!"

"Remember, there is always someone who cares.

You know what they say – the greater the storm, the brighter the rainbow."

"Maybe.."

After that day Loris wasn't as reserved. He was starting to accept his new-found family.

The run is not over yet! Give me your T-shirt!

What are you doing?!

There's always someone who cares, remember? Today – that's me!

Look! Loris is leading the race!

That felt good.

Bravo, Super Brother!

You're like a Super Brother, Cam. This run was your cool idea, and you have the biggest heart ever!

Just one last thing. The author of this book asked me to ask you... Can you leave a review if you enjoy our adventures? Thank you!

Printed in the USA
CPSIA information can be obtained
at www.ICGtesting.com
LVHW070942190324
774814LV00011B/41